This book belongs to

....

LADYBIRD BOOKS

UK | USA | Canada | Ireland | Australia | India | New Zealand | South Africa

Ladybird Books is part of the Penguin Random House group of companies
whose addresses can be found at global.penguinrandomhouse.com.

www.penguin.co.uk   www.puffin.co.uk   www.ladybird.co.uk

Penguin
Random House
UK

First published 2022
001

Licensed by

Printed in China

The authorized representative in the EEA is Penguin Random House Ireland,
Morrison Chambers, 32 Nassau Street, Dublin D02 YH68

A CIP catalogue record for this book is available from the British Library

ISBN: 978-0-241-57563-5

All correspondence to:
Ladybird Books, Penguin Random House Children's
One Embassy Gardens, 8 Viaduct Gardens, London SW11 7BW

MIX
Paper from
responsible sources
FSC
www.fsc.org
FSC® C018179

PePPa's Magical Halloween

It was Halloween, and Peppa and George were dressed up in costumes, ready to go to Magical Halloween Playgroup.

"I'm a magical witch, Daddy," said Peppa. "And George is a magical . . . er, what are you, George?"
"Mon-sta. *Grrr!*" said George.
"Amazing," said Daddy Pig. "And very magical."

"Oh," said Peppa, sighing. "I'm not magical."
"I'm sure you are, Peppa," said Daddy Pig. "Maybe
Magical Halloween Playgroup will help."
"Yes!" cried Peppa.

Peppa and George were very excited when they arrived at Magical Halloween Playgroup. Everyone was dressed in Halloween costumes – even Madame Gazelle!

"Happy Halloween, children!" cried Madame Gazelle, smiling. "And welcome!"

Halloween was Madame Gazelle's favourite day of the year.

"Happy Halloween, Madame Gazelle!" everyone cheered.

The children sat down, and Madame Gazelle told them all about the magical activities they were going to do.

"We will learn to fly on broomsticks, decorate magic wands, eat a Halloween feast, and then –" Madame Gazelle paused – "we will all cast a special magic spell together!"

"Hooray!" everyone cheered.

Magical Halloween Playgroup sounded brilliant!

Hooray!

First, Madame Gazelle helped the children get their broomsticks ready for their flying lesson. Peppa decorated hers with flowers and rainbow ribbons. She even made a little seat for Teddy! "It's so pretty," said Peppa. "Ready to fly, Teddy?"

Next, Madame Gazelle asked the children to grab their broomsticks and line up to go outside.
"Hold on tight as we zoom on our brooms!" she called, leading them on their flight . . .

Peppa and her friends zoomed along, pretending to fly on their broomsticks.

"Watch out for the bats! Now duck under the branch!" cried Madame Gazelle. "Oooh, it's a bit bumpy here! Let's slow down and wave to Mrs Owl."

"*Wheeeee!* I love flying!" shouted Peppa. "It's so magical!"
"I love it, too!" shouted Molly Mole.

Wheeeee!

Then, Madame Gazelle brought the craft tables outside so the children could make magic wands.
"Oooooh!" they cried.
Madame Gazelle told everyone to pick a wand to decorate from the special box.

Oooooh!

"Don't forget to sprinkle on some fairy dust, children," she said.
"We'll need it for our magic spell later."

Once everyone had finished making their magic wands, it was time for the Halloween **feast!**
There were bottles of colour-changing drinks, pretend potions in cauldrons, wobbly jelly bats, toffee apples, pumpkin cupcakes . . .

Munch!

. . . and lots of witch-hat-shaped sandwiches!
"Delicious!" said Mandy Mouse, tucking into a jelly bat.
"Everything tastes yummy *and* magical!" cried Peppa.
Munch! Slurp! Chomp!

Slurp!

Chomp!

When the feast was over, Madame Gazelle asked Peppa and her friends to form a circle, holding their magic wands.

"Now, children," she began, "we have come to the most important activity of the day – casting a **magic spell** together."
"Hooray!" everyone cheered.
"To do this, we **all** need to take part . . . otherwise the spell won't work," said Madame Gazelle.

First the children needed to collect all the ingredients for the spell. Gerald Giraffe found a bag of adventure.

Mandy Mouse found a bottle of kindness.

Richard Rabbit found a pinch of politeness.

George found a
jar of giggles.

And Peppa found
a sprinkle of fun!

Everyone added their magical
ingredient to the big pot.

Madame Gazelle stirred all the ingredients together.
"Wonderful!" she said. "Now, does anyone know
some magic words?"
Peppa put up her hand. "Please!"

Please!

"That's an excellent magic word, Peppa," said Madame Gazelle. "We *must* include that. Any others?"
The children shouted out lots of fantastic magic words . . .

Abracadabra!

Wobbibly-bobbily!

Swishity-swish!

"Madame Gazelle," said Peppa, "how does the spell work?"
"There is a little bit of magic in every one of us," explained
Madame Gazelle. "Now repeat the magic words after me,
and then wave your wands. *Abracadabra, swishity-swish,
wobbibly-bobbily, please!*"

Abracadabra, swishity-swish, wobbibly-bobbily, please!

POOF! Rainbow smoke filled the air, and when it cleared the children saw . . .

POOF!

. . . their parents. They had appeared as if from nowhere!
"Wow!" the children cried. "Sooooo magical!"
"You see, we're *all* magical," said Madame Gazelle.

Wow!

"Yes!" cheered the children.
Everyone said thank you to Madame Gazelle, and then went
home happily with their magical wands and broomsticks.

When Peppa and George got to their front door, Daddy Pig wanted to test out *his* magic. He asked Peppa if he could borrow her wand. Then he pointed it at the front door and said, "Open!" But nothing happened.

"Let me try," said Peppa. She held her wand up and tapped it on the door. *Tap! Tap!* Then she said, "Open, *please*!" And the door opened . . .

Tap!

Tap!

Mummy Pig was waiting inside.
"Don't worry, Daddy," said Peppa, "there is a little bit of magic in all of us. Maybe yours just doesn't open doors?"
"I think Daddy Pig just forgot to say the magic word!" said Mummy Pig.
Peppa and George giggled. "Hee! Hee! Hee!"